FROGGY PLAYS SOCCER

FROGGY PLAYS SOCCER

by JONATHAN LONDON
illustrated by FRANK REMKIEWICZ

PUFFIN BOOKS

For the Dream Team: Sean, Max, Matthew, Travis, B.J., Joseph, Jeff, Rickey, Juan, Goose, Marcos, Dave, Kyler, Bobby, and their coach, Jacqueline Keywood Hammerman
    —J. L.

For José, Kyle, and Anna, champions all.
    —F. R.

PUFFIN BOOKS
Published by the Penguin Group
Penguin Putnam Books for Young Readers, 345 Hudson Street, New York, New York 10014, U.S.A.
Penguin Books Ltd., 27 Wrights Lane, London W8 5TZ, England
Penguin Books Australia Ltd., Ringwood, Victoria, Australia
Penguin Books Canada Ltd., 10 Alcorn Avenue, Toronto, Ontario, Canada M4V 3B2
Penguin Books (N.Z.) Ltd., 182-190 Wairau Road, Auckland 10, New Zealand

Penguin Books Ltd., Registered Offices: Harmondsworth, Middlesex, England

First published in the United States of America by Viking,
a member of Penguin Putnam Books for Young Readers, 1999
Published by Puffin Books, a division of Penguin Putnam Books for Young Readers, 2001

37 38 39 40

THE LIBRARY OF CONGRESS HAS CATALOGED THE VIKING EDITION AS FOLLOWS:
London, Jonathan, date
Froggy plays soccer / by Jonathan London ;   p.   cm.
Summary: Although Froggy is very excited when his Dream Team plays for the city soccer championship, he makes a mistake on the field that almost costs the team the game.
ISBN 0-670-88257-7 (hc)
[1. Soccer—Fiction. 2. Frogs—Fiction. 3. Animals—Fiction.] I. Remkiewicz, Frank, ill. II. Title.
PZ7.L8432Frp 1999 [E]—dc21 98-35725 CIP AC

Puffin Books ISBN 978-0-14-056809-7

Manufactured in China
Set in Kabel

Froggy couldn't sleep.
He looked out the window.
The full moon was rising.
It looked like a soccer ball.
"Tomorrow's the big game!"
he said out loud.
"If we beat the Wild Things
we win the City Cup!"

In the morning,
Froggy was bursting to go.
He pulled on his underwear—*zap!*

Tugged on his
soccer shorts—*zeep!*
Snapped on his
shin guards—*znap!*

Wiggled on his
soccer shirt—*zlim!*
Pulled on his
soccer socks—*zoop!*

And put on his
cleats—*zup! zup!*

called his father.
Froggy's father was
the assistant coach.

"Wha-a-a-a-t?"
"Let's go! We'll be late for the game!"
Froggy flopped outside—*flop flop flop.*

"Remember," said Froggy's dad,
"only the goalie can catch the ball—
and you're not the goalie!

"Now repeat after me:
Head it!
Boot it!
Knee it!
Shoot it!
BUT DON'T USE YOUR HANDS!"

And Froggy sang:
"Head it!

Boot it!

Knee it! Shoot it!
BUT DON'T USE YOUR HANDS! . . ."
all the way to the soccer field.

At the soccer field,
the coach, Max's mother, said,

"We're a *team*.
We're the Dream Team!"
"*Hurray!*" screamed
the Dream Team.

Soon, the game was on!
Froggy was
doing cartwheels.

Froggy was
picking daisies.

Froggy was picking his nose.

The ball bounced
off his chest.
He gave a mighty kick—

and missed the ball.

But Max trapped it and passed it to B.J. who slammed it right into the net—*goal!*

It was one to zero—Dream Team!

Again, the two teams faced off. The whistle blew.
The Dream Team charged down the field toward the Wild Things.
Froggy was tying his shoe.

Froggy's dad was yelling, "Defense! Defense!"
The ball hit Froggy in the head—*bonk!*—
and knocked him down.
He was great at defense.

At halftime,
the Dream Team held the lead.
"Now remember . . . "
said Froggy's dad,
and they all chanted together:
"Head it!
Boot it!
Knee it!
Shoot it!
BUT DON'T USE YOUR HANDS!"

The whistle blew
and the second half started.
A fly circled by.

FRROOGGYY !

called the coach.

"Wha-a-a-a-t?"
"Keep your eye on the—"
Thwap! The ball smacked
him in the eye.

Froggy was mad now.
The Wild Things were stampeding.
And Matthew, the Dream Team's goalkeeper,
was chasing the ball.
Now the goal was unguarded.
This was Froggy's chance!
He leapfrogged over Travis.
He leapfrogged over Matthew.

He leapfrogged over the Wild Things' forward
who was firing the ball . . .

and what a save!
Froggy caught it right before the net.
But, *uh-oh*—he'd used his *hands*!

"Oops!" cried Froggy,
looking more red in the face than green.
He looked so silly, the Dream Team laughed.
But not for long.

The penalty for using his hands was
a free kick at the goal for the Wild Things.
The Wild Things' star forward kicked . . .
and scored. Now it was a tied game!

But it wasn't over yet.
And when there was one minute left
the crowd went crazy.
The clock was ticking.
The ball was coming right toward Froggy.

FRROOGGYY!

yelled his dad.
"Wha-a-a-a-t?"
But Froggy knew what to do.

He jammed his hands
in his armpits.

He stuffed them
in his pockets.

He stuck them in his mouth.

Then he power-kicked the ball
so far down the field
that it bounced over the goalie's head . . .

smack into the goal.
YES!

The Dream Team had won the City Cup!
They shouted and danced.
And Froggy sang:
"Head it!
Boot it!
Knee it!
Shoot it!
BUT DON'T USE YOUR HANDS!—

"except to slap high fives!"—*slap   slap   slap!*